Catchin' Cooties Consuelo

by

Tolya L. Thompson

Illustrated by

Brian Harrold

Savor Publishing House

I dedicate this book to Love. Love captured my heart on a midnight lemon-picking adventure and warmed it under the most magnificent Maui sunset. It finds that one reason to smile when there are thousands of reasons to frown. And the best thing about Love is that I don't have to be perfect to be in its embrace. Love is Michael D. Patten, my husband.   *Tolya L. Thompson*

For Briana and Luke.   *Brian Harrold*

Catchin' Cooties Consuelo
Copyright © 2004 by Tolya L. Thompson
Illustrations by Brian Harrold
Edited by Carol Anderson
Published by Savor Publishing House
Printed in China
All rights reserved
ISBN 0-9708296-3-9
Library of Congress Control Number: 2004090101

Hello there, and how do you do?
I'm Consuelo Truancia and one thing is true:
Going to school just gives me the blues.

All day long I Work! Work! Work!
Where are my bonuses?
Where are my perks?

I'm tired of rules and of sitting in chairs.
I want to be a princess and curl my hair.

Well, I've been thinking, and I've come up with a way
To stay out of school a good number of days.

How will I do it?
It's impossible, you say.
Well, I'm gonna catch a cold,
And I'll catch him today!

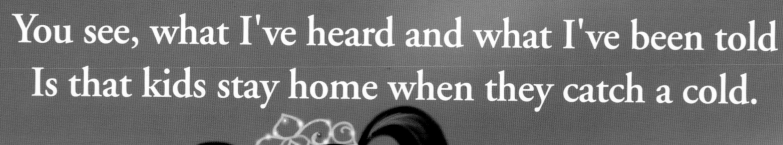

You see, what I've heard and what I've been told
Is that kids stay home when they catch a cold.

Raquel caught one and she's having a ball.
The word is that she'll be out till Fall.

So I'll catch one that isn't very big.
Perhaps he'll have a mustache.
Or maybe he'll wear a wig.

One thing's for sure, he won't be too strong.
He must be weak or things will go wrong.

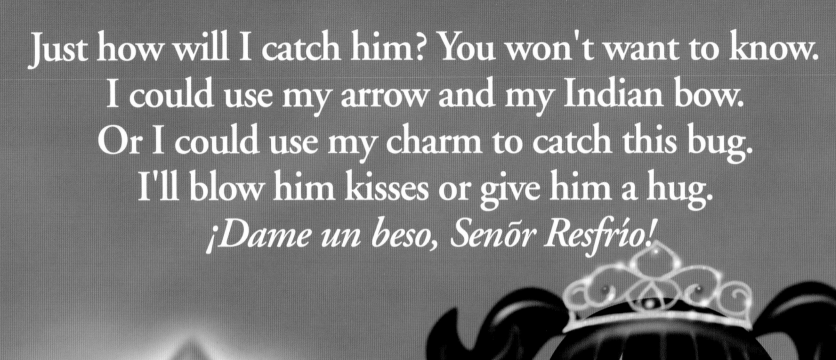

Just how will I catch him? You won't want to know.
I could use my arrow and my Indian bow.
Or I could use my charm to catch this bug.
I'll blow him kisses or give him a hug.
¡Dame un beso, Senõr Resfrío!

The bathroom is where I'll launch my quest.
Yes, this pretty girl is up to the test.
I think the toilet is where I'll begin.
I'll just lift up the lid and reach right in.
Hmm, no cold here.

I'll search through the garbage.
Good thinking on my part.
When Mom leaves the kitchen,
That's where I'll start.

Let's see:
A chicken bone,
An ice-cream cone,
A moldy lime,
An orange with slime,
An egg that's rotten,
And potatoes au gratin.

But no cold.

Could one be hiding deep in the snow?
You never know what the wind might blow.
I'll run outdoors and take a quick look.
I'll bring my pole and fishing hook.
¿Dónde está Señor Resfrío?

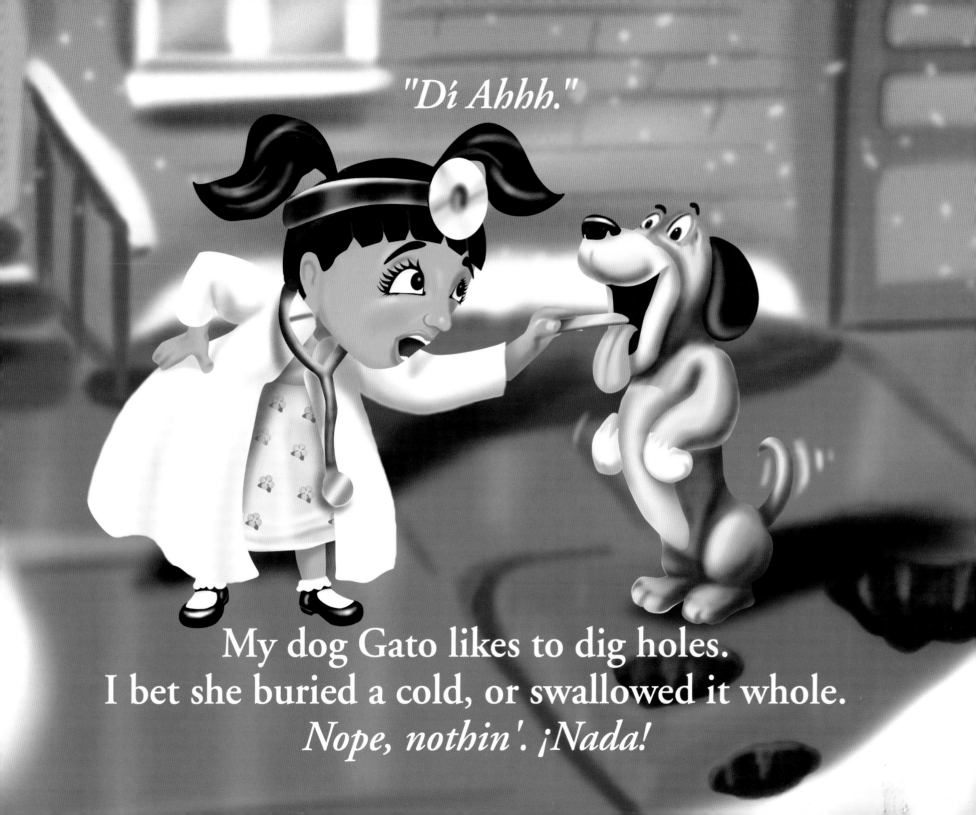

The dirty-clothes hamper is where I'll look last.
I've found nasty things there in the past.

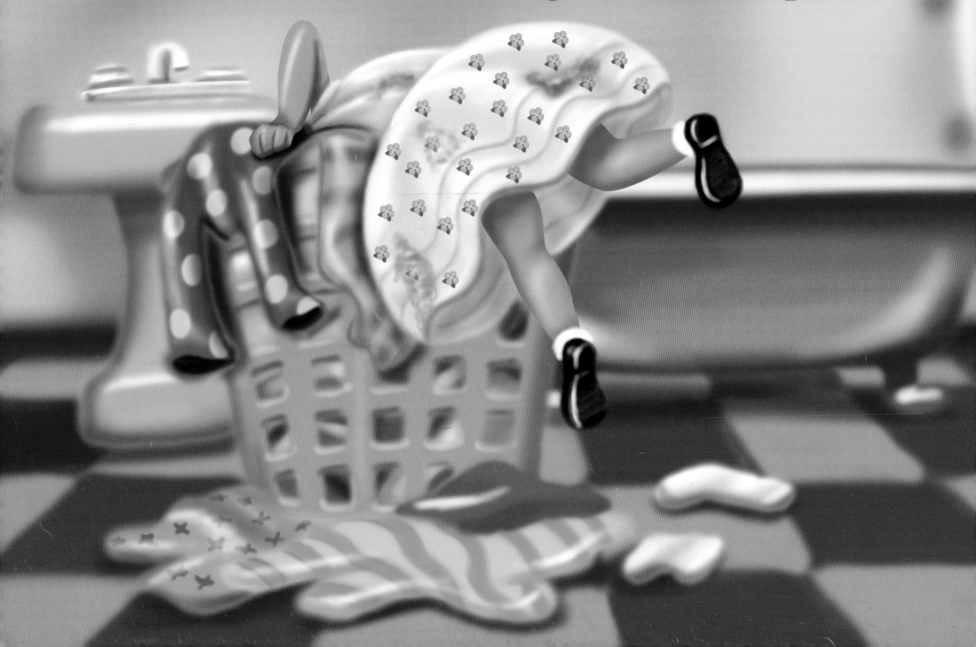

Dirty socks that reek of toe jam,
My brother's pockets filled with ham,
Undershirts covered with dirt,
And underwear with room to spare!
But no cold.

Since Monday I've searched and not a cold have I found.
There seem not to be any colds around.
Ahchoo!

What is this? I don't feel well.
I think my eyes are starting to swell.
Can this be happening? Am I sick?
It's Friday evening. This must be a trick!

Sometimes I feel cold and sometimes I feel hot.
In the middle of my tongue lies a big purple spot.

I cannot swallow. I have a sore throat.
My tonsils are covered in a thick white coat.

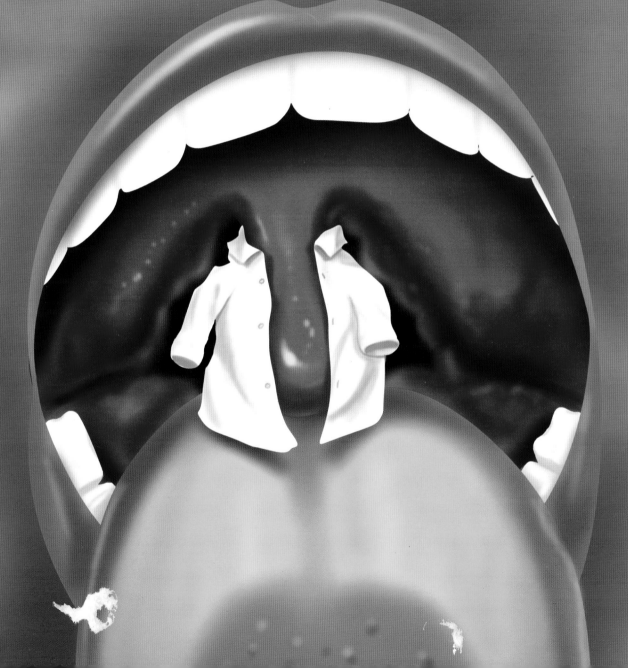

When I close my eyelids they get stuck.
They are crusted over with yellow *yuck!*
My nose is stuffed; I cannot breathe.
There's a big green loogie stuck on my sleeve.

¡Basta, basta, basta! I can't take any more.
My body is aching; my joints are sore.

Ah! Here comes Daddy.
He comes in real handy.
Soup and fluids are what he's brought.
He says the flu is what I've caught.

My flu-catching skills are truly incredible.
Because I caught the flu and the flu was invisible.
It's a good thing I didn't catch a cold or more.
Who knows what a cold would have had in store?

Rest is good when you're under the weather.
So Daddy says to sleep and I'll feel better.

SNORE
SNORE

Buenos días, Consuelo.

Good morning, friends!
Daddies are right in what they say.
I feel much better than I did yesterday.
I feel so good I'll go out and play.

Wait!

Very well, it's understood.
Going to school is always good.
No more playing hooky and searching for colds.
I'll follow the rules and do as I'm told.

Although you know school is tough,
Catching the flu was way too rough!

Consuelo's Smartie

Hey, kids. How many of you out there would do just about anything to avoid going to school? Pretending to be sick is a classic excuse. Well, take it from Consuelo, dodging your responsibilities is never a good idea. From now on, I want you to think of school as an "education vacation" where brain aerobics is your favorite activity. Remember, the more you learn, the more you earn—in knowledge, smarts, and money to burn!

In the story, Consuelo caught the flu, which is medically known as influenza. The flu is a potentially fatal disease that makes you much sicker than the common cold. Both the flu and the common cold are caused by viruses, which cannot be killed with antibiotics. In fact, the use of antibiotics with these conditions can result in serious complications. People who have the flu usually complain of fever, chills, headache, and muscle aches, along with a stuffy nose and watery eyes. In the story, Consuelo was sick for only two days, but in real life the flu generally lasts seven to ten days and sometimes longer. The common cold occurs more frequently in children than it does in adults. Children complain of a scratchy and sore throat, a stuffy nose, watery eyes, and a dry cough. The symptoms of a cold can last from one to two weeks.

Cold and flu viruses are frequently found in places where there are a lot of people in a small space, like schools and hospitals. People often infect themselves by touching surfaces that have recently been contaminated with a virus and then touching their eyes, nose, or mouth. Children often infect one another in school or day care by coughing and sneezing on one another. They then go home and infect their parents. Bed rest and plenty of fluids are the main treatments for both the common cold and the flu. The best prevention for catching a cold is to cover your mouth when you cough or sneeze, wash your hands often, and avoid touching your face. The best prevention against the flu is the flu vaccine. The vaccine is not for everyone, though. Consult your doctor to find out whether you should be vaccinated.

The flu is particularly dangerous for children who suffer from asthma, HIV, cancer, or other chronic illnesses. Parents, if your child is having difficulty breathing, shows signs of dehydration, suffers from exhaustion, or has a high fever that is not relieved by medication, please seek medical attention right away.